This paperback edition first published in 2014 by Delere Press LLP

Illustrations ⓒ Li Kexin, Ivy
Layout ⓒ Chan Yin Wan
Text ⓒ Juli Crockett

*   *   *

First published in 2014 by
Delere Press LLP
Block 370G Alexandra Road
#09-09 Singapore 159960
www.delerepress.com
Delere Press LLP
Reg No. T11LL1061K

ISBN   978-981-09-2655-7

[or, the whale]

Juli Crockett

with illustrations by Ivy Maya

[THE FOREWARNED;
OR, A PRODUCTION HISTORY]

For some point of reference, it might be useful to know that [OR, THE WHALE] was first staged at California Institute of the Arts in Valencia, California in the year 2001. Composed by Jeremy Zuckerman and borne out of our mutual obsessions with music & language (and language as music,) we set out to create an opera of spoken words (and parts of words) partially inspired by the extended vocal technique work of Trevor Wishart. The cast consisted of 24 men representing three Ahab's (and one more Dark Ahab), several crews of Starboys, some Seadogs, a Pip, and a Fedalah. In the round with two tiers of audience members peering into the skeletal massive ship, it was a spectacular production, a great success in many ways, and in other ways an utter failure for Jeremy and me, as we were not able to realize at all what we had intended in the realm of sonic composition. Much of the spectacle of spectacular was achieved thanks to the profound talents of scenic designer Melissa Ficociello, lighting designer Peter Ksander, costume designer Angela Bright, and Jeremy's soundscapes (infuriating to him, to be reduced to such, but such it was, under the circumstances.)

In 2004, a crew of 21 theater persons known as TENT gathered together in Portland, Maine to live and work for one month. In residence at St. Lawrence Arts and Community Center, they developed a performance piece adapted from the text of [OR, THE WHALE] entitled

OH SWEET CAPTAIN, OR THE AHAB STOMP. IT WAS REPORTED THAT AFTER MANY ARGUMENTS A WHALE WAS EVENTUALLY INCLUDED IN THE PIECE, (WHO DIED, BLOWN UP ON THE OREGON COAST ACTUALLY), AND THUS MAINTAINED THE DICTUM THAT AT THE END OF THE OPERA EVERYONE HAS TO DIE.

IN 2014 *[OR, THE WHALE]* WAS REVIVED WITH THE POOR DOG GROUP FOR A STAGED READING AT THE BOOTLEG THEATER, IN PREPARATION FOR PUBLICATION. THE PIECE WAS PRESENTED WITH A CAST OF 4 MEN, REPRESENTING 3 MELVILLE'S (AND/OR AHAB'S) AND A PIP. IN SOME WAYS, THIS MINIMAL PRODUCTION CAME CLOSER TO MORE FULLY REALIZING THE SONIC INTERESTS THAT HAD OBSESSED JEREMY AND ME YEARS BEFORE, COMING AT IT, HOWEVER FROM A WILDLY DIFFERENT ANGLE.

IT SEEMS TO ME THAT IN REALIZING ANYTHING, WE FAIL.

IDEAS SIMPLY CAN'T MAKE THE JOURNEY FROM THE REALM OF THOUGHT TO THE GROSS WORLD OF OBJECTS WITHOUT SOME DIMINISHING TRANSMUTATION. IN THIS FAILING, HOWEVER, ANOTHER THING ENTIRELY OCCURS, BEYOND OUR WILLING. AND THIS IS WHERE MY ART HAPPENS — BEYOND THE AUTHORSHIP OF THE EGO, IN CONCERT WITH CHAOS.

OR SOMETHING LIKE THAT.

- JC

YESTERDAY
LOS ANGELES

⟦PROLOGUE⟧

⟦or⟧ to indicate
an alternative,
equivalent or
substitutive,
approximation
or uncertainty,
alter of other,
either or
whether, before
or before,
sink or swim,
to lessen or
abate, in three
or four years
(are ye with
me or against
me?) Akin to OHG
(the unnamable)
alter of OE (the
unutterable.)
One that does
a (specified)
thing. Sink or
swim, feet or
fins, heaven or
hell, all is
well. Out of the
sight of land.

High time to get
to sea.

⟦and⟧ usually
after or often
after, or
sometimes. Used
to join. (*Used
to join.*) A
consequence of
come, go, try.
Infinite purpose,
and the rest, and
so forth, and on.
An individual:
standing, as a
habit, in point
of fact, a former
state, of a loss,
a greater loss,
little or no
loss connects
the mere fact,
intended for one
person existing
separate,
particular,
indivisible. Take
part, the lowest.

High time to get
to sea.

[alt] Born New
York City.
Died New York
City. 1819.
1891. Revived
when no longer
alive. 1891.
1819. Etymology,
neither fish
nor foul.
Inversely, died
in obscurity.
Novelist,
poet, sailor,
(poet), customs
inspector. Third
of eight and
weak of I. (Good
morning.) Good
morning, it is.
What shall we do
today?

Today we will
fail. Up to the
ankles, up to the
knees, up to the
waist. Dogs on
the beach. Over
the shoulders,
over the chin,
over the mouth
and nose.

High time to get
to sea.

I. [REMEMBER THE MYTH OF AHAB]

What do you know of him? What have ye heard? What do you know of our Captain except that he is a mad Captain and that his madness meant death to his crew? Have ye heard what happened to him off Cape Horn all those years ago when he lay like dead for three days and three nights in the belly of hell till he was vomited up upon dry land? *He saw the opening maw of hell, with endless pains and sorrows there~;*

~ *Moby Dick, Chapter 9*

Have ye heard of the deadly scrimmage with the Spaniard in front of the altar at Santa and how he spat in the silver calabash offending all the island gods and the wrath and the prophecy upon his very soul?

Have ye heard of the curse that all little boys grow up, except one, and how he was cursed at birth with a singular beauty (and double cursed to love only his self same self) and how he first saw himself in a pool of still water and swore to love the ungraspable phantom till the day till the day he drowned?

Have ye gone down to the springs of the sea or walked in the unfathomable deep? Have ye comprehended the vast expanse of the world? Tell me all this, if you know.˜

~ JOB 38:16-18

Have ye heard how he loved the floating thing and how his loves seem'd always to be out of reach, out of view, out of the sight of land? And how in reflecting so long upon the mirrored sea he himself became a reflection, and his reflection, reflecting, made way for another, and another, and another…

Have ye heard it said that wonderfullest things are ever the unmentionable and deep memories yield no epitaphs? In landlessness alone resides the highest truth, shoreless, indefinite as˜ - - -

~ *Moby Dick*, Chapter 23

Ahab, Ahab, and Ahab. All for one and one with none.

So, better is it to perish in that howling infinite, than be ingloriously dashed upon the lee, even if that were safety.~

Glimpses do ye seem to see of that mortally intolerable truth; that all deep earnest thinking is but the intrepid effort of the soul to keep the open independence of her sea; whilst the wildest winds of heaven and earth conspire to cast her on the treacherous, slavish shore.~~

Have ye heard that there be no shadows at night and no reflections neither and only in the fullest moons will ye be seeing either?

And everyone knows this part…

Everyone knows about the leg.

~ *Moby Dick*, Chapter 23
~~ *Ibid.*

How the leg was taken.

How the leg was lost.

How he only has one leg and how the other was taken from him according to the prophecy. Lost at sea; ripped from he.

Cursed to love only his self same self and that which he could not have.

Cursed with reflections and the ungraspable phantom.

Cursed with floating feelings and phantom limbs.

And methinks we have hugely mistaken this matter of life and death. Methinks that what they call my shadow here on earth is my true substance. Methinks that in looking at things spiritual, we are too much like oysters observing the sun through the water, and thinking that thick water the thinnest of air. Methinks my body is but the lees of my better being. In fact, take my body who will, take it I say, it is not me.~

~ Moby Dick, Chapter 7

Only the fish that loved the land too much
drowned on that other stuff that we take
for our each day and every day. Turn it all
around; in the air the fish will drown,
in water men go down, and only drown'd men
drown.

And what is the sound of failure? Tell me,
if you know. What is the sound of utter
despair?
What is the sound of ambition?
What is the sound of

                    falling short?
What is the sound of

                    potential?
What is the sound of

                    defeat?
What is the sound of

                    a dying dream?

What is the sound of the unbearable deep?
And what is the sound of one leg floating?

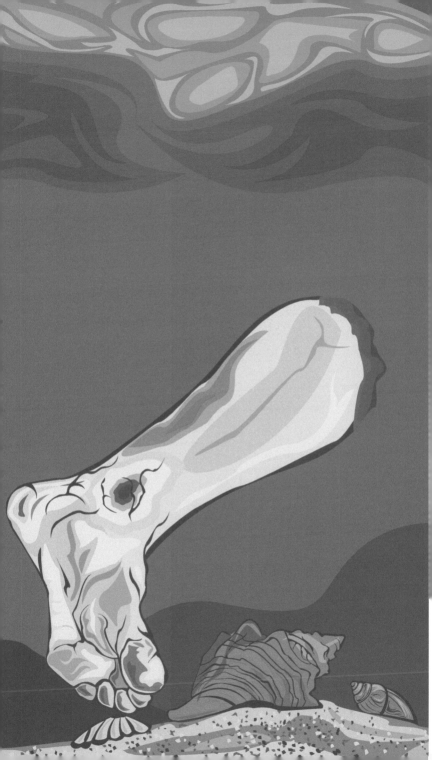

II. [REMEMBER HOW IT ALL BEGAN]

Remember how it all began,
Always the same again and again,
There once was a man, who lost his leg,
Instead of a leg now he walks on a peg.
He takes one step and that's a leg,
He takes one step and that's a peg,
A leg and a peg and a leg and a peg,
Oh how he misses his little leg.
(Oh how he misses, oh how he misses,
Oh how he misses his little leg.)
He thought about the missing leg,
Until it drove him out of his head
And then he split himself in three,
All of 'em Ahab, Captain to me.

So here's the story:

THERE ONCE WAS A MAN WHO LOST HIS LEG AND HE THINKS ABOUT IT ALL THE TIME AND CRIES ABOUT IT AND IT REALLY TEARS HIM UP INSIDE. THIS LOSS. THIS MISSING LIMB. HE FOCUSES ON THE LOSS -- THE LEG -- ALL THE TIME. HE LOOKS OUT OVER THE OCEAN AND THINKS, "WHERE IS THAT LITTLE LEG?" SUCH A LITTLE LEG IN SUCH A BIG OCEAN, IT COULD BE ANYWHERE. IT COULD HAVE BEEN SWALLOWED BY A BIG FISH, OR PECKED TO PIECES BY BIRDS, OR IT COULD HAVE SUNK AND IT MAY BE LYING IN THE VERY BOTTOM OF THE OCEAN, ON THE OCEAN FLOOR. BUT, METHINKS IT FLOATS.

(HE CAN STILL FEEL HIS LEG, JUST LIKE, AS IF, IT WAS ON HIM STILL, EXCEPT HE GETS A FLOATING FEELING. AND THAT'S HOW HE KNOWS IT'S STILL OUT THERE.) HE CAN FEEL IT FLOATING.

SO, THERE IS THIS FEELING BETWEEN MAN AND LEG; THE LOSS, THE UNFATHOMABLE LOSS OF THAT WHICH WAS HIS, HIM, PART OF HIM, ABSOLUTELY HIM, SOMETHING WHICH, HE THOUGHT, COULD NE'ER BE TAKEN (FOR HOW CAN ONE TAKE ONESELF AWAY FROM ONESELF?)

MOST FOLKS DON'T SPEND A LOT OF TIME THINKING, "WHAT IF I LOSE A PART OF MYSELF" BUT ANYONE WHO KNOWS SOMEONE WHO HAS LOST A PIECE OF THEIR SELF THINKS ABOUT IT. FOR EXAMPLE, IF YOU KNEW A MAN WHO LOST HIS FINGER CUTTING AN APPLE, YOU MAY THINK TO YOURSELF, WHILE CUTTING AN APPLE, OR JUST USING A KNIFE, "I HOPE I DON'T LOSE A FINGER." (YOU SEE WHAT I'M SAYING?) BUT MORE LIKELY YOU DON'T SPEND A LOT OF TIME HOPING YOU DON'T (OR THINKING YOU MIGHT) LOSE SOME PART OF YOURSELF.

HOWEVER, IT HAPPENED, AND THE RESULT WAS A CHASM, A SPLIT, A BIG GAP, WHICH MADE THE WHOLE

WIDE WORLD NOTHING BUT DISTANCE; OBSTACLES BETWEEN HIM AND HIMSELF (HIMSELF BEING THE WHOLE HIM WHICH WASN'T WHOLE ANY MORE.) WHAT HE IS NOW ONLY A PART OF WHAT HE WAS.

HOW COULD A LITTLE LEG TAKE SO MUCH AWAY? WELL, IT DID.

AND THERE IS POINT A AND THERE IS POINT B BUT ALL HE CAN SEE IS THE SPACE IN BETWEEN. BUT MAYBE THIS DISTANCE MADE HIM BIGGER THAN HE EVER THOUGHT HE COULD BE, BECAUSE MAYBE, ALL THE SPACE BETWEEN HIM AND HIMSELF AND THE MILES AND MILES OF OCEAN BETWEEN HIM AND THE REST OF HIM COUNTED AS A KIND OF HEIGHT, SO THAT, IF THE LEG WAS ON, HE WAS A MAN OF AVERAGE SIZE AND AVERAGE STATURE, BUT WHEN THE LEG IS OFF, COUNTING ALL THE DISTANCE BETWEEN WHERE HE IS AND WHERE IT'S AT, HE COULD BE, SAY, 3,000 MILES FROM HEAD TO TOE, OR MORE, (DEPENDING ON WHERE HE IS AND WHERE IT'S AT.)

AND IT MAY BE SAID THAT "WHAT IS TO BE, WILL BE" AND IT COULD ALSO BE SAID THAT "THIS BE DESTINY" AND IT COULD ALSO BE SAID THAT "THE LEG WORKS IN MYSTERIOUS WAYS" AND THAT "THE LEG GIVETH AND THE LEG TAKETH AWAY" BUT IT COULD ALSO QUITE POSSIBLY BE SAID THAT THERE WAS AN ACCIDENT. A TERRIBLE ACCIDENT WHEREIN A MAN LOST HIS LEG, AND SINCE THE MAN AND LEG USED TO BE ONE WITH EACH OTHER, PERHAPS THE BEST WAY TO RESOLVE THIS PROBLEM WOULD BE TO RETURN THINGS TO THE WAY THINGS WERE. (TO GET IT BACK.) GET BACK WHAT HAS BEEN LOST.

BUT THAT SOUNDS DANGEROUS, DOES IT NOT? IN THE TIMES OF FORWARD TO GO BACK ALWAYS SEEMS THE WRONG DIRECTION. PERHAPS HE SHOULD SEEK A BETTER LEG, A DIFFERENT LEG AND NOT THE VERY SAME LEG HE LOST. (MOVE ON.) MOVE ON TO THE

NEXT BEST LEG. THE OLD LEG HAS BEEN OUT TO SEA FOR A LONG, LONG, TIME AND IT COULD BE ANYWHERE. (SUCH A BIG SEA.)

AND HOW ARE WE TO FIND HER? TWO THIRDS OF THE WORLD IS COVERED IN WATER AND HE SAYS SHE'S FLOATING THERE AND WE MUST FIND HER. BUT, TO FIND SOMETHING OUT AT SEA IS VERY DIFFICULT; ESPECIALLY SOMETHING SMALL, THAT DOESN'T GLOW OR MAKE A SOUND. (AND AFTER ALL, SHE COULD'VE DROWNED, SUNK STRAIGHT DOWN.)

NO, SHE FLOATS!

AND WE WILL SPEND THREE YEARS AT SEA LOOKING FOR THE FLOATING THING, IF IT TAKES THAT LONG, AND WE'LL STAY LONGER IF WE DON'T SPOT HER. WE'RE OUT TO SEA UNTIL HE'S GOT HER.

HE SAYS SHE'S OUT HERE, AND WE HAVE TO BELIEVE HIM. WHAT ELSE ARE WE GOING TO BELIEVE? OUT HERE, UNDER HIS COMMAND, SEARCHING FOR THE FLOATING THING AND ALL WE KNOW IS THAT HE THINKS IT FLOATS BECAUSE HE FEELS IT FLOATING IN HIS BONES WHICH MEANS HIS BODY WHICH MEANS HIS BRAIN WHICH MEANS HE THINKS HE FEELS IT FLOATS.

(HE BELIEVES IT FLOATS.)

AND THERE'S THE RUB. HE BELIEVES. AND THERE YOU ARE.

HE BELIEVES, WE BELIEVE.

AND WE ALL HAVE TO BELIEVE BECAUSE THAT'S WHAT KEEPS IT FLOATING AND IF IT SINKS WE SINK AND THERE'S THE RUB. WE DON'T WANT TO SINK. AND THAT'S WHY WE'RE HERE AND HE'S GOT US.

AND WHY WOULD A MAN WHO DOESN'T WANT TO SINK
SIGN ON TO A SHIP TO SEARCH FOR A LITTLE LOST
LIMB?

WELL, PERHAPS I'D RATHER SINK THAN STAND.

AND I'D RATHER SWIM THAN SINK.

AND I'D RATHER FLOAT THAN SINK OR SWIM OR
STAND.

AND MAYBE WHEN WE FIND THIS FLOATING THING
IT WILL TELL US SOMETHING OF WHAT IT IS
LIKE TO FLOAT FOR YEARS AND YEARS WITHOUT
SINKING. OR SWIMMING. OR STANDING. IS THAT
NOT THE DREAM? IS THIS NOT A DREAM?

ALL I DO ALL DAY IS LOOK FOR THE FLOATING
THING, AND THIS CAN MAKE A MAN TIRED. AND
THREE YEARS AT SEA CAN MAKE A MAN LONELY. AND
THINGS THAT AREN'T CAN SEEM TO BE WHEN ONE IS
FAR, FAR OUT TO SEA.

THE SUN WENT DOWN AN HOUR AGO,
I WONDER IF I FACE TOWARDS HOME.
IF I LOST MY WAY IN THE LIGHT OF DAY,
HOW SHALL I FIND IT NOW NIGHT HAS COME?

AND WHAT ELSE?

THERE'S A MILLION THINGS THAT MAKE ME HATE
THIS LIFE OF OURS: 1, 2, 3, 4,
                            5, 6, 7, 8,
                            9, 10, 11, 12,
                            13, 14, 15, 16,
                            17, 18, 19, 20, 21,
                            22, 23, 24, 25, 26,
                            27, 28, 29, 30, 31,
                            32,
                            33...

THE DAY
TO DAY
TO DAY
TO DAY
TO DAY
TO DAY
TO DAY...

LET THE MATTER DROP.
LET THE LOG LINE ROT.

~ OLD SONG. QUOTED IN RUDYARD KIPLING'S *THE LIGHT THAT FAILED*, CHAPTER XIII

And if we never backward go,
Borne home on ocean's breast,
But find among the caves below
A sailor's place of rest;
Still 'ere we close our eyes
And drift beneath the depths of blue,
We'll think upon the floating thing
And how we died for you,
Sweet captain, how we died for you.~

And sometimes we sleep and sometimes we dream
that we've found the floating thing and our
Captain is whole and we're floating home and
all is one and our work is done and the ship
is safe and she sails herself home.

~ Source: *The Norfolk Girls*, Sea Shanty. See: Shanty

And the tide rolls in
And it rolls out again,
And the sea is a wicked old wicked woman.
There's a hole in the bottom of the sea.
The sailor's life for me.~~

And isn't it strange that the sound of sleeping is so much like the ocean when you listen to the breathing. In and out. Out and in. And tomorrow will be so natural. The sun is already coming up. And you keep it there. Morning to ye, shipmates, morning. Morning it is. (Sweet Captain...)

And here's where the story begins. (Again.)

Wait.

~~ Traditional. This text also appears in the song "Ahab's Leg" (Evangenitals)

III. [ENTER AHAB]

IN COMES THE OLD ARCHETYPE AHAB ICON SEA
CAPTAIN MYTH OF A MAN WITH THE ONE LEG THE
OTHER TAKEN BY A…

"HEAVILY WALKING THE DECK."~

HE LOOKS DOWN INTO THE OILY DEEP AND WHAT
DOES HE SEE? CAN HE SEE HIS REFLECTION
ON THIS MOONY NIGHT? (OF COURSE.) AHAB IS
CURSED WITH REFLECTIONS. HE GAZES DOWN INTO
THE MOONY DEEP AND HE SAYS WHAT ALL LOVERS
SAY. (AYE, ME.) HE SIGHS. HE SIGHS! OH,
SIGH AGAIN, SWEET CAPTAIN. AND HE DOES. AND
HE SAYS HIS SMOKING NO LONGER SOOTHES SO
HE'LL SMOKE NO MORE. (I'LL SMOKE NO MORE.)
I WILL SMOKE NO MORE, FOREVER.

AND HE DROPS HIS PIPE INTO THE BLACK NIGHT
SEA AND IT IS SAID, "THE FIRE HISSED IN
THE WAVES" AND "THE BUBBLE THE SINKING
PIPE MADE" AND METHINKS THIS IS BEAUTIFUL,
BUT NOT SO BEAUTIFUL AS THE SAD MAN
ABOVE. *FORLORN, FORLORN, THE LONELY CAPTAIN
MOURNS THE LOSS OF HIS LITTLE LEG.*

AND HIS EYES LIFT UP FROM THE DEEP, AND HE
LOOKS IN THE DIRECTION OF THAT DISTANCE
WHICH HE FEELS PULLING AT HIS HEART, LIKE
A FISHHOOK IN HIS HEART. AND MAYBE HE EVEN
PUTS A HAND ON HIS HEART AND SIGHS. AYE,
ME. OR PERHAPS HE FEELS THE FISHHOOK IN SOME
OTHER PART, THE OLD SEA-SALT SEA CAPTAIN OF
THE ONE LEG (THE OTHER BEING THE MISSING
ONE THAT WAS LOST A LONG, LONG TIME AGO.)

LOST?

*FORLORN, FORLORN, (EACH NIGHT THE LEG THE
LONELY CAPTAIN MOURNS.)*

~ *MOBY DICK*, CHAPTER 28

He sighs, he sighs, and stares into the deep, the dark. And he looks the look — searching for the secret of the inky black, which hides his little leg in its night sea.

Night Sea.

He speaks, he swoons, "Aye, me." He sighs. What's that? Old sea-salt, speak again. He swears, he swoons, "Oh where oh where oh where oh where?" and echo, echo, echo…

And he whispers, "Where are you?" and he speaks of his lady. (Oh my lady, oh my love.) Look what happened. I miss you. (Me?) "Aye, me." Forlorn, forlorn…

Perhaps you prefer it out there on your own. Rather than being a piece of me, you are the leg that floats in the sea. Rather than just one of two that a mere man walks on — you float, you flow. But I will find you. (But what if, perchance, you don't want to be found?) Perhaps you prefer your loneliness. Perhaps loneliness is something that little legs like much more than men. I don't know. Let me know. I'm ready to get you. (Or, let go).

Let go? Let you float and I let go? Go on with the one leg and I make do and this part of a man, which I am, becomes the whole man. (But I am not a whole man.) I am part of a man. Two thirds of the globe is covered with sea and floating in that sea is a piece of me. Hundreds of bones in my foot alone are gone — adrift — alone — alone. She floats, she floats, she flows, she flows. (Sometimes they stay and sometimes they go.)

SHE WON'T GO DOWN, SHE WILL NOT DROWN. I
KNOW. I CAN FEEL HER AS SHE FLOATS. I CAN
FEEL HER. AS SHE ROLLS, I ROLL. AS SHE
FLOATS, I FLOAT. I CAN FEEL HER HERE BUT
NOT THERE. EVERYTHING MOVES OUT THERE. AND
SHE MOVES TOO.

ALONE, AFLOAT, ADRIFT, AWRY, AFEARED, AFOUL,
AWAY.

THE DAY TO DAY TO DAY TO DAY TO DAY TO DAY
TO DAY.

(THERE IS A COLD WIND THAT BLOWS THROUGH
THIS BOOK.)

IV. ⟦FINDING AND FORGETTING⟧

EVERYBODY KNOWS YOU CAN NEVER FIND A
GODDAMN THING WHEN YOU'RE LOOKING FOR IT.
EVERYBODY KNOWS THAT YOU CAN'T FIND THE
THING THAT YOU'VE LOST WHEN YOU'RE LOOKING
AND ONLY WHEN YOU STOP LOOKING CAN ANYTHING
BE FOUND. BUT THAT'S NOT FINDING, DAMMIT,
THAT'S JUST… WHATEVER. NOT FINDING.

REMEMBER THE RULE OF FINDING AND FORGETTING?

IF SOMETHING IS LOST THEN THAT SOMETHING
CAN ONLY BE FOUND IF IT IS LOOKED FOR.
IF YOU DON'T LOOK FOR IT THEN YOU'LL FIND
SOMETHING ELSE, FORGETTING WHAT THE LOST
THING WAS AND THINKING THAT THE FOUND THING
IS AS GOOD AS WHATEVER IT WAS THAT WAS LOST.

BUT YOU'LL NEVER KNOW FOR SURE BECAUSE
ACCORDING TO THIS EQUATION YOU MUST FORGET
THE FIRST THING TO FIND THE SECOND, AND
HAVING SUCCESSFULLY FORGOTTEN THE FIRST
THING YOU ARE BY NO MEANS ABLE TO MAKE A
COMPARISON BETWEEN SOMETHING FORGOTTEN AND
SOMETHING FOUND. AND EVEN IF THE SECOND
THING WERE THE SAME THING, THE VERY SAME
THING, AS THE FIRST, HOW WOULD YOU KNOW?
YOU FORGOT THE FIRST.

(AH, BUT YOU NEVER REALLY FORGET THE FIRST
THING.)

THIS IS THE GAME? PRETEND TO FORGET (SO
THAT YOU CAN FIND) BY PRETENDING THAT YOU
AREN'T LOOKING ANY MORE? HOWEVER, METHINKS
IF YOU SUCCESSFULLY PRETEND TO FORGET (AND
THIS IS A GAME FOR ONE PERSON ONLY, SO IT IS
YOUR SELF-SAME-SELF THAT YOU MUST PRETEND
TO FORGET) METHINKS THIS IS THE SAME AS
FORGETTING.

And when they say, "thou hast forgotten thyself" perhaps this suggests that your self-same-self is not the first, but the second, or even the third and that the first was forgotten long ago, never to be found because the search was called off in order to pretend to forget so that thou might find.

And what do you think? Do you think this self is better than the first self? Perhaps you will pretend to believe so because what is the good of believing the first was the best when you are the second, or the third, in the great chain of finding and forgetting.

And your self-same-self (the individual whom you think of when you thinks of you) the individual, then, is a splintered, shifting thing. Always, in all ways, pretending to forget so that thou may cease seeking (but not cease finding.) And there you are; with one or two or three (or even four) self-same-selves that you forgot and found and forgot and found again.

And what if you keep forgetting the real thing you were looking for and instead keep finding something else? And how can one remember to seek if one forgets what is intended to be sought? (Can a forget beget a seek, before the sought is forgot?)

And who said you had to forget to find it? And who came up with the idiotic idea about pretending to forget?

Nothing sinks before its time! (That is what we like to believe.)

ONLY DROWNED MEN DROWN. IT'S AS SIMPLE AS
THAT.

AND MAYBE, IT SEEMS TO ME, IT MAY HAVE
BEEN, PERHAPS, THE PROBLEM WITH ALL OF THIS
IS THAT THE PIECE KEEPS BEING FORGOTTEN SO
THAT IT MAY BE FOUND, YET THE PERSON IS
ALWAYS IN MIND, SO MAYBE, IT MAY BE, IT IS
ALL WRONG AND BACKWARDS AND THAT IS WHY THE
PERSON IS FOUND AGAIN AND AGAIN AND AGAIN
(AND AGAIN) BUT THE PIECE, THE MISSING
PIECE, (FORGOTTEN) IS NEVER FOUND. BECAUSE
DOESN'T IT SEEM TO MAKE A KIND OF SENSE
THAT TO FIND, THOU MUST SEEK, AND TO SEEK
THOU MUST FIND (IN THE MIND) A FAITH OF
SOME KIND IN WHAT (SEEKING) THOU HOPES TO
FIND? FOR THERE ARE BUT FEW, BUT THERE ARE
A FEW, WHO SEEK FOR SEEKS SAKE AND FIND BY
FAITH ALONE. BUT FEW THERE ARE.

AND WHEN YOU HAVE FORGOTTEN SOMETHING YOU
DID NOT MEAN TO FORGET, AND SUDDENLY --
YOU REMEMBER -- BUT YOU REMEMBER TOO LATE,
DO YOU NOT FEEL A STRANGE SORT OF SINKING
INSIDE?

REMEMBER, THIS SHIP IS GOING DOWN;
AND ALL THESE MEN ARE GOING TO

DROWN.

But wouldn't it be nice if before that sinking, there could be a sign? One last chance to seek and find and never mind the pretending to forget or the second thing or the third thing (or even the forth) but time to find the original thing. (To get it back.)

And when you remember something, long forgotten, in the nick of time, to stop the sinking, first you search on the inside (thinking) for some memory (ah, memories) to help you recognize the real thing when you see it. And then you search on the outside. And where to look for it? Where to do your seeking? (Well, where did you see it last?)

Floating. In the big moving ocean where nothing stays still.

V. [THE SIGN OF THE SEADOGS]

THE SEA IS A WICKED OLD WOMAN~ AND IT IS A
WICKED GENERATION THAT DEMANDS A SIGN.~~

DEMANDING A SIGN IS A SIGN OF THE TIMES, A
SIGNAL, A SYMPTOM, A SICKNESS.

THE ONLY SIGN THAT WILL BE GIVEN IS THE SIGN
OF THE SEADOGS AND THE SIGN WILL COME "IN
THE USUAL WAY" WITH THE SOUND AND THE LOOK
AND THE NODDING COMPREHENSION OF IT ALL.

AND WHAT 'TIS A SEADOG?

THE SEADOG IS TO THE SIREN AS THE SIREN
IS TO THE SEAL, AS THE SEA-SALT IS TO THE
SEA (AS MY MEMORIES ARE TO ME.) IT IS,
ALWAYS WAS, AND FOREVER SHALL BE. 'TIS THE
MAN 'TWAS AWAY FROM THE TOO LONG AT SEA
TILL HE FORGOTTETH THE SEA WAS THE SEA AND
HE WAS HE AND IT ALL BLENDED TOGETHER.
(INDEFINITELY.) FOR, WITH EACH DROP OF WATER
THE SEADOG SPEAKS. HE KNOWETH ALL THINGS
THAT DISRUPT THE DRIFT OF THE DEEP. KNOWS
WHEN SAD CAPTAINS ADD THEIR TEARS TO THE
SEA, WHEN YOUNG BOYS FALL O'ERBOARD TO
ENDLESS SLEEP, ALL THE LANDLESS ATROCIOUS
DEEDS, ALL THE SECRETS OF THE BRINY DEEP,
AND *WHERE OH WHERE OH WHERE COULD SHE BE,
THE LEG THAT FLOATS UPON THE SEA.*

AND WHAT ARE YOU LOOKING FOR? (THE LEG.) AND
WHAT DO YOU MEAN BY THAT? FOR THERE ARE MEN
WHO SEEK FOR WHAT A THING IS AND MEN WHO
SEEK FOR WHAT A THING MEANS AND I WONDER
WHICH ONE IS WHICH AND WHICH ONE ARE YOU?

~ 'THE MEN OF THE SEA' IN *THE LIGHT THAT FAILED.*
~~ *BOOK OF JOB*

Do you know my story?
(Yes, I know your story.)

Do you understand?
(Yes, I understand.)

Can you stop this pain?
(Yes, I can.)

No, no, no, no. She beckons, she beckons,
and I follow, I flow.

And how do you know? (*Noah's flood's not
over, more than half the globe is covered
in water.*)

All the water, every drop; salt lakes and
sweat and tears and sea. And the sea has
a bottom and the sea has a top, and this
is very deep, trust me. And there are two
options: start at the bottom and rise to
the top, start at the top and sink to the
bottom.

How long can you hold your breath?

...

...

...

...

VI. 【PIP】

PIP?

PIP!

WHO'S SEEN PIP?

Pip's missing.

Ding, dong, ding. Gone. Long gone.

Five feet high. Looks cowardly.

Jumps ships. Hold his hand, you won't let go. No reflection in his eyes. No reflections at all. Seen him? What? Pip? Pippen by nickname, Pip by abbreviation, brought back to life by resuscitation, flew straight up to the bottom of the sea, AKA ascension, AKA visitation, AKA annunciation, not to be confused with enunciation, man-rope by avocation, peg-leg by necessitation, hang-dog look, last seen holding a tam-bour-ine? Heard a thump and he went jump. Shame overboard! If he sinks, he's a coward. If he floats, he's a coward. Better to be a boot. A buoy. A boy. Five feet high, hang-dog, water-logged, and cowardly! Jumped from a boat once — seen him? Here he this instant stood; I stand in his air, -- but I'm alone. Seen him? Ho! There's his arm just breaking water. Five feet high, dead eyes, lost soul, can't pay the bills, and cowardly! Seen him? No! Well then, fill up again, captains, and let's drink shame upon all cowards! I name no names. Put one foot upon the table. Shame upon all cowards. Tread on me, sir; I ask no more.~

(There is something about that boy.) There is nothing worse than nothing, where once there was something. Jerk him, Tahiti. Jerk him off. (There is something about that boy.) There is always a choice. One or the other. This or that. Sink or swim. To look or not to look, that is your question. (You'll miss him when he's gone, but he won't be gone for long.) There once was a man who lost his leg. It should be remembered that nothing is known. Voglio. Voglio. Voglio. Voglio il voler mio. I will. I will. I will. I will have my way. (There is something about that boy.) Now then, Pip, we'll talk this over; some unknown conduits from the unknown worlds must empty into thee!~

"Left alone, in the ocean, where the awful lonesomeness is intolerable, in the middle of such a heartless immensity, Pip's ringed horizon began to expand around him miserably."~~

And everybody knows this one. The truest song 'ere written on the deep blue sea. Sing it with me.

~ *IBID.*
~~ *IBID.*

SHE GOES:

DOWN
DOWN
DOWN
DOWN
DOWN
DOWN
DOWN
DOWN
DOWN
DOWN
DOWN
DOWN
DOWN
DOWN
DOWN
DOWN
DOWN
DOWN
DOWN
DOWN
DOWN
DOWN
DOWN
DOWN
DOWN
DOWN
DOWN
DOWN
DOWN
DOWN
DOWN
DOWN
DOWN
DOWN
DOWN
DOWN
DOWN
DOWN
DOWN
DOWN

Down

Down

Down

Down

Down

Down

Down

Down

Down

Down

Down

Down

Down

Down

Down

Down

Down

Down

Down

Down

Down

Down

Down

Down

Down

Down

Down

Down

Down

Down

Down

Down

Down

Down

Down

Down

Down

Down

(AN ENDLESS GLISSANDO DOWNWARD.)

VII. ⟦THE FOG DOG⟧

SOMETIMES, IN A FOG, ON THE HORIZON, THERE IS SEEN, A POINT OF LIGHT, THROUGH THE MIST, AN APPARITION, UNSTAINED, SUCH A CLEAN WORLD, PURE LIGHT, WHICH EVERYTHING BECOMES WHEN IT IS FOLDED NEATLY INTO ITSELF, FOR SAFEKEEPING, IN THE FINAL MOMENT, A TENDER SITUATION, SUCH A DELICATE WORLD, OPENING UP, SPOTLESS GEOMETRY, A TEMPORARY ETERNITY, A FLOATING GLOBE, SUCH A CLEAN WORLD, A TENDER SITUATION.

THIS REMINDS ME OF SOMETHING I'VE BEEN TRYING TO REMEMBER, OR FORGET, ONE OR THE OTHER, EITHER OR WHETHER, BEFORE OR BEFORE, SINK OR SWIM. AND WHAT DO YOU UNDERSTAND SO FAR? ARE THERE WORDS INTO THOUGHTS, OR FEELINGS INTO WORDS? THEN COMES MEMORY. AND WHAT WAS IT THAT HAPPENED JUST A MINUTE AGO? JUST A MINUTE, LET ME REMEMBER. LET ME RECOLLECT. REMIND ME. WHAT WAS I LOOKING FOR? THIS FEELS LIKE WHAT I'M LOOKING FOR. I LOOK DEEP DOWN AND I DO BELIEVE. I SEE. (I COULD SHOW YOU A PERFECT WORLD, BUT IT ONLY LASTS FOR A SECOND.)

IS AHAB, AHAB? IS IT I OR HE WHO LIFTS THIS ARM? IS THIS ME, YOU? DO I MOVE OR AM I MOVED? IS THERE ANY DIRECTION OR ALL THINGS TO A COMMON POINT? IS THERE ANY DISTANCE OR IS IT ALWAYS THERE? DO I BEGIN AND END HERE, RIGHT HERE?

LET ME TELL YOU A SECRET. YOU WILL NEVER KNOW, IN THE END. THERE IS NO OTHER, EITHER OR WHETHER, THERE IS NO AFTER, ONLY BEFORE. THIS IS THIS AND THIS IS IT. THERE IS NO OR. NO ONE WILL REMEMBER WHOM YOU WERE BEFORE OR BEFORE. NOT ONE PERSON HAS A SINGLE MEMORY OF AN AHAB WITH **TWO LEGS.**

— *MOBY DICK*, CHAPTER 132

⟦RELEASEMENT⟧

The Perfervid
Gladiators,
Melancholy
Atheism, Moral
Intransigence,
Pathologically
Destructive
Resentment,
Failure and
Annihilation,
Forlornest Of
Mankind, Arrant,
All-Grasping,
Intermeddling,
Monopolizing,
Heathenish,
Accursed, Damned,
Everlasting
Slaughter,
Miserable,
Morbid,
Maniacal,
Saturnine,
Struck By
Lightning,
Sorrow Made Man.

[RELEASEMENT]

The Advocate, The
Alpha and Omega,
The Bridegroom,
The Chosen One,
Eldest of Many
Brothers, The
First and
the Last,
Firstborn of
All Creation,
Glory, Hope, Head
of Every Man,
Image of the
Unseen, Light
of the World,
Living Bread,
The Man, The
Morning Star,
Only Son of the
Father, Perfect
Copy, Rising Sun,
Radiant Light,
Ruler of All,
True Vine, The
Way, Word Made
Flesh.

IX. ⟦AHAB'S DEFENSE⟧

Those who die in the city will be food for the dogs, and those who die in the country will by food for the birds,˜ and those who die at sea will be food for the fish, and everybody eats every other body, like waves overtaking waves, we come and go, come and go. And if one boy is in the way of a man's destiny, that boy should know when it is time to go. Let a drowned man drown. Let him go down.

~ *1 Kings* 21:24

(We didn't suspect that the person was really drowning, even though they were saying that they were. They said they were drowning, but they didn't say it like they were really drowning.)

"Death is only a launching into the region of the strange Untried; it is but the first salutation to the possibilities of the immense Remote, the Wild, the Watery, the Unshored; Seat thyself sultanically among the moons of Saturn, and take high abstracted man alone; and he seems a wonder, a grandeur, and a woe. But from the same point, take mankind in mass, and for the most part, they seem a mob of unnecessary duplicates."~

Remember the Myth of Ahab? Ahab is, always was, and forever shall be, the mad captain of the one leg whose madness means death to his crew.

There is a wisdom that is woe; but there is a woe that is madness. We have found the source and he is a riddle, and the riddle contains the source and the source is Madness. There lies my puzzle; but thine is greater. Thou knowest not how came ye; certainly knowest not thy beginning; I know that of me, which thou knowest not of thyself.

~ *Moby Dick*, Chapter 107

All your oaths are as binding as mine; heart, soul, and body, lungs, and life, old Ahab is bound.~ You seek that which I seek. You seek for me. Are me. What is mine, shall be mine. I say what I say. I do not sleep, I die. I am the Captain of my Ship.

(I'd rather nothing were true, than to see your truth.)

Shall this crazed old man be tamely suffered to drag a whole ship's company down to doom with him? Yes — it would make him the willful murderer of all these men and more, if this ship come to any deadly harm; and come to deadly harm, my soul swears this ship will, if Ahab has his way. Aye, 'tis said the men have vow'd thy vow; sayest all of us are Ahab. I stand alone here upon an open sea, with two oceans and a whole continent between me and law. On this level, Ahab swings. Would I be a murderer, then, if~~ —

If you were doing a puzzle, and you got down to the very last piece and found it missing, would you not look for it? Would it not drive you a little crazy, this missing piece? Would it not drive you a little crazy that when you look at the picture you've made, apparently, aberrantly incomplete, all you see can see is a hole. The main point of focus, in the sea of pieces, is a hole. And you can see straight through the whole picture through that one little hole.

(Let the matter drop.)

~ *MOBY DICK*, CHAPTER 119
~~ *MOBY DICK*, CHAPTER 123

I WILL NOT LET THIS GO! NEED I, SHALL I, REMIND YOU ALL? THERE ONCE WAS A MAN WHO LOST HIS LEG. AND WHAT IS LOST SHOULD BE FOUND, IS THAT NOT THE WAY OF ALL THINGS? LOSS BEGETS ALL LOOKING. NOTHING BEGETS NO THING. FOR A MAN WHO IS NOT ALL IN ONE PIECE IS PERPETUALLY PARALYZED BY TRYING TO GO TWO DIRECTIONS AT ONCE.

THERE IS POINT A AND POINT B, AND WHY WOULD YOU WANT TO KNOW THESE THINGS? ALL THINGS LEAD TO THAT COMMON POINT, THE END, AND ALL THINGS CONVERGE AT THAT MOMENT. ALL FORCE PULLS US TOWARD, WHILE ALL FORCE DRIVES US AWAY. (THAT WOULD BE THE EQUATION OF THE DAY TO DAY TO DAY.) AND THIS CREATES AN ENORMOUS AMOUNT OF PRESSURE. A DELICATE BALANCE. THE CRUSHING WEIGHT THAT KEEPS THE WATER INSIDE THE OCEAN. DOGS ON THE BEACH. A TENDER SITUATION.

THE FACT OF THE MATTER IS, THE TWO CANNOT BE ONE, NOR CAN THREE BE ONE OR FOUR BE ONE (IS IT NOT HARD ENOUGH FOR ONE TO BE ONE?) IN FACT, THERE IS NO CERTAINTY THAT ONE IS ONE. IN FACT, THERE IS NO CERTAINTY AT ALL.

IN THE FINAL MOMENT, WHEN THE DAY IS DONE, WHEN THE CAPTAIN BECOMES ONE, WHEN IT'S ALL COMPLETE, AND HE TURNS INTO HIMSELF, HE TURNS INTO HIMSELF, THAT IS TO SAY, IN THE END, A PERFECT MOMENT, PURE LIGHT, A CLEAN WORLD, A COMPLETE MAN, A FLOATING GLOBE, A TEMPORARY ETERNITY, THE STARTING POINT, BEGINNING OF ALL GEOMETRY, SUCH A CLEAN WORLD, EVEN IF IT ONLY LASTS FOR A SECOND, 'TIS LONG ENOUGH, FOR MINE EYES HAVE SEEN, AT THE PERFECT MOMENT, A POINT OF LIGHT, ON THE HORIZON, A CLEAN WORLD, COMPLETELY TRANSPARENT, AS IS EVERYTHING, AS IS IT ALL, ALTER OF OTHER, EITHER OR WHETHER, BEFORE OR BEFORE, SINK OR SWIM, FEET OR FINS, TO BURST INWARD, TO UNDERGO VIOLENT COMPRESSION, TO COLLAPSE INWARD FROM OR AS IF FROM, DOGS ON THE BEACH, EXTERNAL PRESSURE, THE ACT OR ACTION OF BRINGING TO [OR] AS IF TO A CENTER; INTEGRATION.

AND IN THE FINAL MOMENT, ALL YOU ARE IS ALL YOU WERE, YOU REMEMBER. AND MEMORY IS NOTHING BUT AIR, AND ALL YOU ARE.

I am the Captain of my ship.
I am the Captain of my ship.
I am the Captain of my ship.
Sail away. Sail away. Sail away.

AND WHO IS AHAB? "THE CAPTAIN" (AH YES)
"CAPTAIN" OF WHAT? "OF MY SHIP." AND THERE'S
THE RUB. "MY" SHIP. FOR THOU CANST NOT EVEN
BE THE CAPTAIN OF THYSELF, DEAR AHAB. FOR
THOU HAS LOST THYSELF (TO SOME DEGREE, IS IT
NOT SO?) FOR THE LEG WAS YOURS AND SHE IS LOST
AND IF THIS SHIP BE YOURS THAN PERHAPS SHE BE
LOST AS WELL. AND IF THIS INDEED BE YOUR SHIP,
DEAR CAPTAIN, WHAT IS IT TO US? COULD YOU NOT
BE THE CAPTAIN OF "OUR" SHIP? THEN WE COULD
JOIN OUR DESTINIES, RATHER THAN RIDING ON THIS
BORROWED BOAT TO YOUR DESTINATION (WHICH,
WE ARE AFEARED, MAY BE A MOST MELANCHOLY
SPOT.) FOR ALL NOBLE THINGS ARE TOUCHED WITH
MELANCHOLY, JUST AS ALL MEN TRAGICALLY GREAT
ARE MADE SO THROUGH A CERTAIN MORBIDNESS.
AND HERE IT COMES, THERE IS ALWAYS A PATTERN
TO THINGS AND A MAN WHO KNOWS NOT CHANGE
KNOWS ONLY AGAIN AND "OH, NOT AGAIN." AND IF
THIS BE HIS SHIP THAN THIS SHIP BE LOST. JUST
LIKE HIS LEG. JUST LIKE US ALL. AND THEN
THERE IS THE FINAL REFRAIN. AND THAT NEEDS
NO EXPLANATION, BECAUSE IT IS NOT ANYTHING
THAT CAN BE EXPLAINED. 'TIS A FEELING, AND A
FEELING 'TWILL REMAIN.

I AM THE CAPTAIN OF MY SHIP.

~ *MOBY DICK*, CHAPTER 16

X. ⟦ALONE (AT LAST)⟧

AND WHEN I SAY ALONE, WHAT I MEAN IS, HE TOILED ALONE AND IN THE DARK. NOT EASILY EXPLAINED OR UNDERSTOOD. THE WORDS OF THE WISE AND THEIR DARK SAYINGS. WIDESPREAD IGNORANCE, LACK OF PROGRESS. AS, WE ARE ALL IN THE DARK CONCERNING HIS PLANS. AS, PLANS HATCHED IN THE DARK. AS, DARKS AND LIGHTS ARE BOTH NECESSARY. AS, WATER IS NECESSARY TO LIFE. THAT WHICH MUST BE DONE. LABOR. TOIL. DRUDGERY.

BELOW THESE WATERY PASTURES LIE THE ANSWERS TO ALL THINGS, WHICH WE CAN ONLY GAZE UPON AND WONDER AT THEIR UNSTEADY REFLECTION. THE IMAGE THAT I SEE BENEATH IS THE MOODY MOVING IMAGE OF MY STATE OF BEING. AND ALL THESE WORDS WHICH FLOW AND STREAM ARE BUT A FEEBLE ATTEMPT TO PUT A LABEL ON A FEELING. TO TRANSFORM A FEELING INTO AN IDEA INTO A WORD INTO A MEMORY INTO SOMETHING I CAN RECALL AT A LATER DATE AND SAY 'OH YES, REMEMBER WHEN AND HOW IT WAS AND DOESN'T IT FEEL SO NICE THAT IT ALL GOES ON AND ON AND THAT IT ISN'T ALL MEANINGLESS?' BECAUSE I HAVE ASSIGNED A WORD AND A MEANING TO EVERY *THING*. AND EACH EXPERIENCE HAS ITS CATEGORY AND EACH MEMORY IS IN ITS CABINET AND MY LIFE CAN BE WRITTEN DOWN IN A SERIES OF ANECDOTES AND OCCURRENCES THAT WILL MAKE MEN SMILE AND FROWN AND LAUGH AND CRY AND I LIVE AND I DIE IN AN ENTIRELY RATIONAL MANNER.

I SHALL PROCEED TO MY LOGICAL CONCLUSION.

AND IN THE END, WHAT IS A MAN IF HE MAKES NO
SENSE?

AND WHAT IS THE SOUND OF FAILURE? TELL ME,
IF YOU KNOW.

WHAT IS THE SOUND OF UTTER DESPAIR?
WHAT IS THE SOUND OF FALLING SHORT?
WHAT IS THE SOUND OF DEFEAT?
WHAT IS THE SOUND OF A DYING DREAM?
WHAT IS THE SOUND OF THE UNBEARABLE DEEP?

XI. [THE LEG IS FOUND]

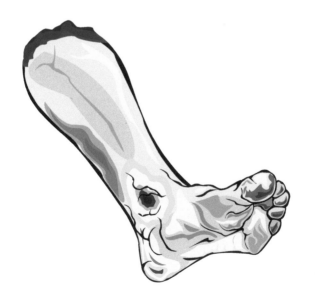

I WANT TO TELL YOU A STORY ABOUT A MAN WHO
LOST HIS LEG. HE THINKS ABOUT IT ALL THE
TIME. HE TALKS TO IT, AND SOMETIMES IT TALKS
BACK. (THE PHANTOM LEG.)

WHAT SHALL WE DO TODAY? TODAY WE WILL FAIL.
UP TO THE ANKLES, UP TO THE KNEES, UP TO THE
WAIST. DOGS ON THE BEACH. OVER THE SHOULDERS,
OVER THE CHIN, OVER THE MOUTH AND NOSE. SINK
OR SWIM, FEET OR FINS.

THE LEG WAS FLOATING BY: A GREAT AND STRONG
WIND CAME, RENDING MOUNTAINS AND SHATTERING
ROCKS BEFORE IT; BUT THE LEG WAS NOT IN
THE WIND; AND AFTER THE WIND THERE WAS
AN EARTHQUAKE; BUT THE LEG WAS NOT IN THE
EARTHQUAKE; AND AFTER THE EARTHQUAKE, FIRE,
BUT THE LEG WAS NOT IN THE FIRE; AND AFTER
THE FIRE A FAINT MURMURING SOUND…˜

CAN ANY HUNGER EVER TRULY BE GRATIFIED?
TOMORROW AND TOMORROW, OR IN BUT A FEW HOURS,
ANOTHER HUNGER COMES, IS ALREADY COMING.
PERHAPS THE VERY SAME HUNGER RETURNS. NEVER
LEFT. NEVER BETTER. ALL FULLNESS LEADS TO
EMPTINESS, AND EVERY IS TURNS TO NOT.

BID FAREWELL TO THE NATURE OF MAN. NO
THING. NOT ANYTHING. NONE AT ALL.
33,
32,
31, 30, 29, 28,
27, 26, 25, 24,
23, 22, 21, 20,
19, 18, 17, 16,
15, 14, 13, 12,
11, 10, 9, 8,
7, 6, 5, 4,
3, 2, 1...

~ *1 KINGS* 19: GOD'S WORD TO ELIJAH

EVERYTHING HAPPENS AT THE RIGHT TIME.
EVERYTHING HAS ITS OWN PLACE WHERE IT'S NOT
ANY PROBLEM TO BE THE WAY IT IS. AND HERE IT
IS…

USED TO JOIN. (USED TO JOIN.) A CONSEQUENCE
OF COME, GO, TRY. INFINITE PURPOSE, AND THE
REST, AND SO FORTH.

AND THEY
        ALL

    GO

          DOWN.

"...THEN ALL COLLAPSED, AND THE GREAT SHROUD OF THE SEA ROLLED ON AS IT ROLLED FIVE THOUSAND YEARS AGO."~

~ *MOBY DICK*, CHAPTER 135, LAST LINE.

THE END.

(WAIT.)

〖An After Word〗

Dear Reader,

This is a play. Do with it what you will.

I have left out anything that could limit an openness to the possibilities. These are the words — at least some of them. You might look to the source material for many more, and the sources behind that, and on and on and then some, and soon we are arrived at the infinite sea of words, words, words.

Much has already been said about the meaning and themes and mythology of Moby Dick. What I would add is that there is a preoccupation — a love affair — with the sound of language, as a musical thing, in concert with the word. A balancing act ensues, lest the word destroy the music by becoming mired in the limitations of meaning — numbing the senses to the inherent, primal, and cultural content of the sound itself — or, at the other extreme, musicality engulfs the word, drowning its will to mean. I work to allow sound to be a sensation as well as a signifier, simultaneously; to allow a word to be itself and also its sounds. That is a real trick which has proved impossible save for brief moments.

Yet, those moments are sublime.

-JC

This morning
Los Angeles

JULI CROCKETT IS A PLAYWRIGHT, THEATER DIRECTOR, RETIRED (UNDEFEATED) PROFESSIONAL BOXER AND AMATEUR CHAMPION, ORDAINED MINISTER, DOCTOR OF PHILOSOPHY (SUMMA CUM LAUDE), SONGWRITER, AND LEAD SINGER OF THE GENRE-DEFYING BAND THE EVANGENITALS. HER WORK HAS BEEN PERFORMED IN NEW YORK, LOS ANGELES, MAINE, AND AT THE EDINBURGH FRINGE FESTIVAL. PUBLISHED WORKS INCLUDE *VOID CREATION: THEATER AND THE FAITH OF SIGNIFYING NOTHING* (ATROPOS PRESS) AND EXCERPTS OF A NEW PLAY, *SAINT SIMONE*, APPEAR IN THE COLLECTION *I MIGHT BE THE PERSON YOU ARE TALKING TO* (PADUA PLAYWRIGHTS PRESS). SHE LIVES IN MONTECITO HEIGHTS, CA WITH HER HUSBAND, COMPOSER MICHAEL FELDMAN, THEIR SON THELONIOUS, A TORTOISE, AND THE FAMILY CAT, ŽIŽEK.

IVY MAYA IS AN ILLUSTRATOR, BORN AND TRAINED IN SINGAPORE. SHE HAS PARTICIPATED IN JOINT EXHIBITIONS WITH OTHER SINGAPOREAN ARTISTS, IN THE EXHBITIONS INCLUDING *PIPLATCHKA MAKERINGS,* AND *TIGER SHOW* BY THE CAT WELFARE SOCIETY. SHE IS TATTOO CRAZED, AND LIKES TO BE SURROUNDED BY FRUITY PEOPLE SUCH AS THE GOOD FOLKS AT DELERE PRESS, AND WRITER JULI CROCKETT.

Lightning Source UK Ltd.
Milton Keynes UK
UKHW050651130219
337140UK00001B/35/P